THE MOUNTAIN JEWS AND THE MIRROR

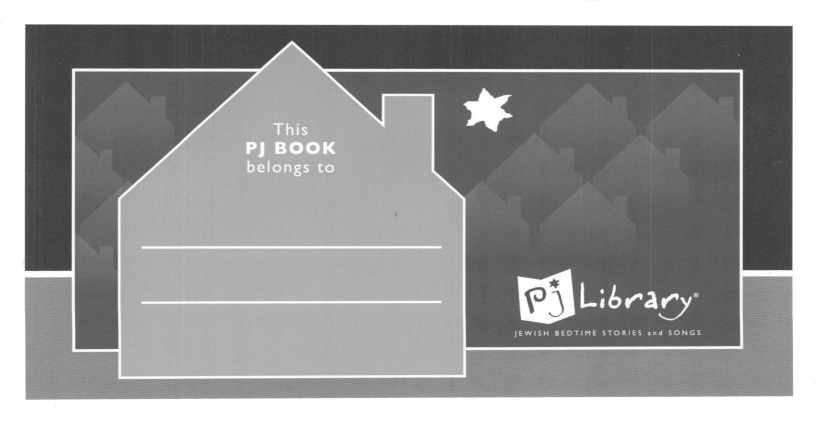

This **PJ BOOK** belongs to

_____

_____

PJ Library®

JEWISH BEDTIME STORIES and SONGS

KAR-BEN PUBLISHING
A division of Lerner Publishing Group, Inc.
241 First Avenue North
Minneapolis, MN 55401 USA
1-800-4-KARBEN

Website address: www.karben.com

Main body text set in Brioso Pro Medium 16/20.
Typeface provided by Adobe Systems.

Library of Congress Cataloging-in-Publication Data

Feuerman, Ruchama King.
    The mountain Jews and the mirror / by Ruchama King Feuerman ; illustrated by Polona Kosec and Marcela Calderon.
        pages cm
    Summary: When a newly married couple from a small Moroccan village moves to the city of Casablanca,
the mirror on their wardrobe causes much confusion, as they each think their spouse has married someone new.
    ISBN: 978-1-4677-3894-1 (lib. bdg. : alk. paper)
    ISBN: 978-1-4677-3896-5 (pbk.)
    [1. Marriage—Fiction. 2. Mirrors—Fiction. 3. City and town
life—Fiction. 4. Jews—Morocco—Casablanca—Fiction.
5. Humorous stories.]
    I. Kosec, Polona, illustrator. II. Title.
    PZ7.F434Mo 2015
    [E—dc23   2014029040

PJ Library Edition ISBN 978-1-4677-3895-8

Manufactured in China
2-47560-16033-4/12/2019

101929.2K2/B0744/A7

THE MOUNTAIN JEWS AND THE MIRROR

RUCHAMA KING FEUERMAN

ILLUSTRATIONS BY
POLONA KOSEC
AND MARCELA CALDERÓN

KAR-BEN
PUBLISHING

In a faraway village in the Atlas Mountains of
Morocco, Estrella and Yosef got married. *Mazal bueno!*
All the mountain Jews threw them a big party.

But the new young couple worried. How would they feed and support themselves? Yosef made money selling nuts and raising sheep, but it wasn't enough for the two of them.

Then good news came. Estrella's uncle wrote to her parents, "Send the young couple to Casablanca. Yosef will work in my carpet shop. They can rent a small apartment close by."

Estrella and Yosef clasped their hands. An answer to their prayers! But then Estrella's face clouded. "How can we leave our village? We know nothing about the big city."

"Don't worry," said Yosef as they packed their few belongings.

In Casablanca, Estrella's uncle and cousins prepared an apartment. They added a rickety table, a blue chair here, a yellow chair there, two beds, blankets, pots and utensils. The only thing missing was a wardrobe for clothes.

When Estrella and Yosef arrived, they stared in amazement. Two whole rooms just for them! So much furniture! Smooth, shiny floors, not like the dirt floors in their village.

Soon, Yosef said goodbye to his wife and left for his new job at the carpet shop. Estrella walked to the market to buy vegetables.

She gazed at the other women walking past with their baskets, as the vendors called out, "Watermelon, cheap! Sweet tomatoes!"

"These women are so beautiful," thought Estrella with a pang. "Much more beautiful than I am."

While Estrella shopped, her cousins were lugging a wardrobe, step by step, up to the new couple's apartment. How heavy it was! It was the finest they could find. They placed it opposite the door, where it could be seen and admired by anyone who entered.

Estrella returned home with
her vegetables, eager to make the
special salad Yosef loved.

She opened the door to her
apartment, and her eyes fell upon
a strange, beautiful woman!

Estrella screamed and ran down the stairs, back into the street. She threw her arms up. "*Weelie, weelie,* my husband has taken another wife! Oh, help me! What should I do?"

"Ask the rabbi," said a woman, pointing her toward the synagogue where the rabbi studied the holy Torah all day.

Estrella rushed to the synagogue and told the rabbi her terrible story. "We have just moved here, and suddenly my husband thinks he can take another wife?" Her dark eyes flashed. "I won't put up with this!"

Her voice dropped to a whisper. "The new wife is more beautiful than I." And she wept bitter tears.

The old rabbi stroked the hairs of his white beard, trying to make sense of this strange story. He was a wise man, though not very worldly—he spent his time in the synagogue and kept far from the outside world.

Meanwhile, Yosef had spent his morning selling carpets to proud, handsome city men who smiled at him with pity and said, "Ah, a mountain Jew. I can tell just by looking at you."

Yosef returned home for lunch, his shoulders sagging. He had never felt so low. What was he compared to these fine fellows? Just a simple Jew from a mountain village.

Still, he put on a smile for Estrella and opened the door to the apartment.

Surprised, he saw a handsome man standing in the middle of the room! Yosef gasped and shut the door.

"*Ay ay ay*, Estrella has found another husband!" He, too, rushed to the synagogue to seek advice from the rabbi.

"My wife has married another man!" Yosef told the rabbi. "Does she think, just because she found someone handsomer than I, that she can set me aside"—he snapped his fingers—"just like that?"

"Hmmm," said the rabbi. A wife with two husbands. A husband with two wives. What craziness was this? "I must come to your apartment and see for myself what the trouble is," he said.

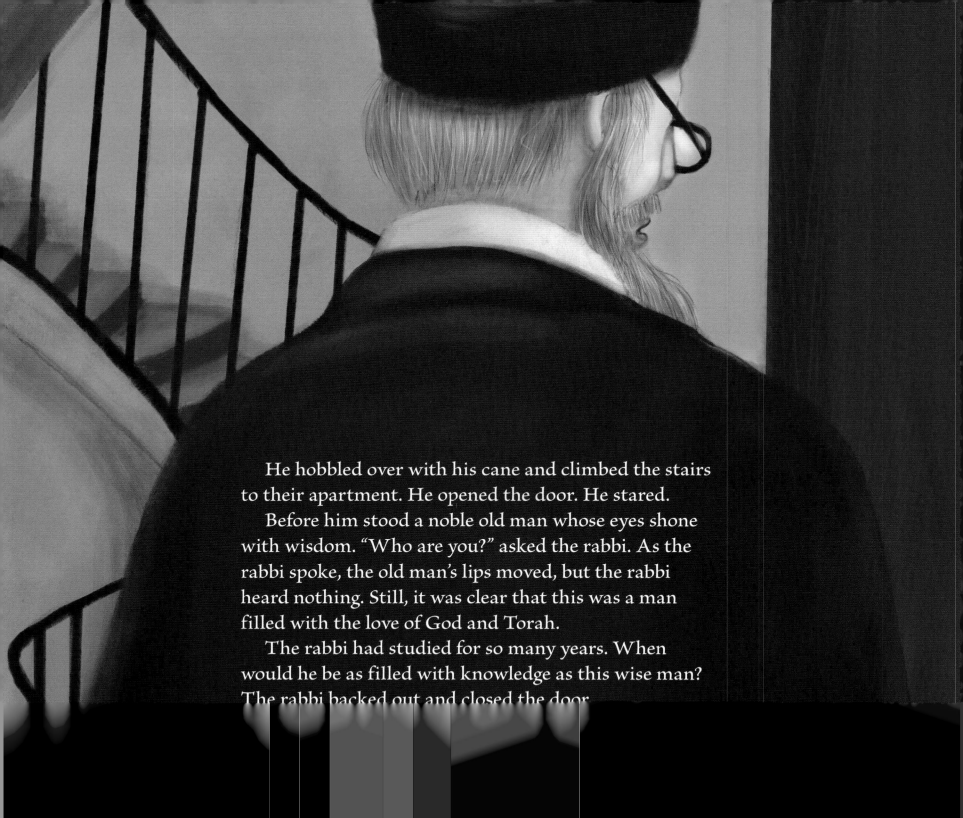

He hobbled over with his cane and climbed the stairs to their apartment. He opened the door. He stared.

Before him stood a noble old man whose eyes shone with wisdom. "Who are you?" asked the rabbi. As the rabbi spoke, the old man's lips moved, but the rabbi heard nothing. Still, it was clear that this was a man filled with the love of God and Torah.

The rabbi had studied for so many years. When would he be as filled with knowledge as this wise man? The rabbi backed out and closed the door.

The community gathered outside, the women surrounding Estrella, the men huddled around Yosef.

"Well," said the rabbi, "you don't need me to handle this problem after all. There is already a rabbi upstairs."

People looked at one another in confusion. "Wait!" exclaimed a young man. "It's the mirror! That's what they've been looking at!"

Estrella and Yosef stared. They had never heard of a mirror.
"But what about the beautiful woman?" Estrella sputtered.
"That's you," the women told her. "Your own reflection."
"But who was that tall, handsome man?" Yosef demanded.
"That's you," the men explained.

"Dear husband," Estrella said to Yosef shyly, "I am beautiful, am I not?"

"Oh, Estrella," Yosef said, kissing her fingertips. "You are as beautiful as the stars!" Then he ducked his head. "Dear wife, I think you married a handsome man, no?"

"Goodness, Yosef!" she said. "You are a finer sight than rain in the desert!"

They beamed at each other. Hand in hand, they walked up the stairs to their new home.

The rabbi chuckled to himself. "Of course, a mirror!" He thought for a moment. "So that wise man filled with the love of Torah was—*me*?"

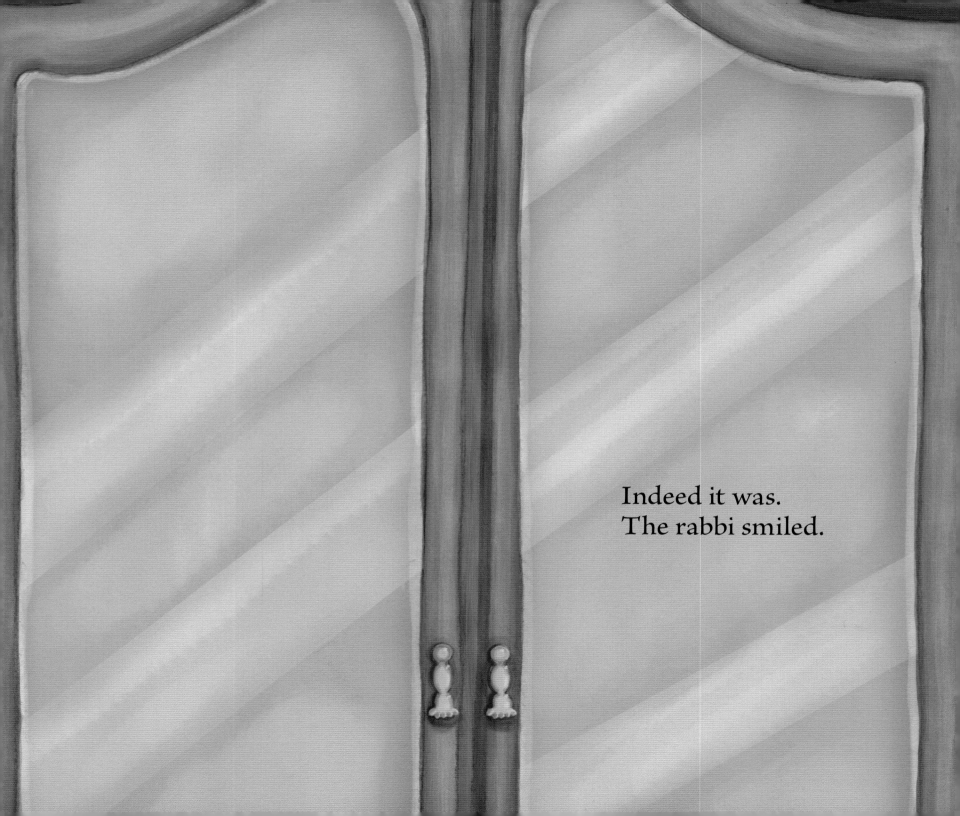

Indeed it was.
The rabbi smiled.

RUCHAMA KING FEUERMAN, born in Nashville, grew up on the East Coast and at seventeen bought a one-way ticket to Israel to seek her spiritual fortune. She is the author of two adult novels, *Seven Blessings* and *In the Courtyard of the Kabbalist*. This is her first children's book. She lives in Passaic, New Jersey.

POLONA KOSEC illustrates with acrylics but also enjoys drawing with other materials as well as creating some of her illustrations digitally. Paper and colored pencils were the two things that took her mind off sweets when she was a little girl. She has a Master of Arts from the Academy of Fine Arts in Ljubljana. She lives in Ljubljana, the capital city of Slovenia.

MARCELA CALDERÓN lives in Argentina, where she works as a freelance illustrator. She likes the smell of graphite, the scent of wood pencils, the sound of chalk on paper, acrylic textures, and the feel of the eraser. Basically, she loves to draw.

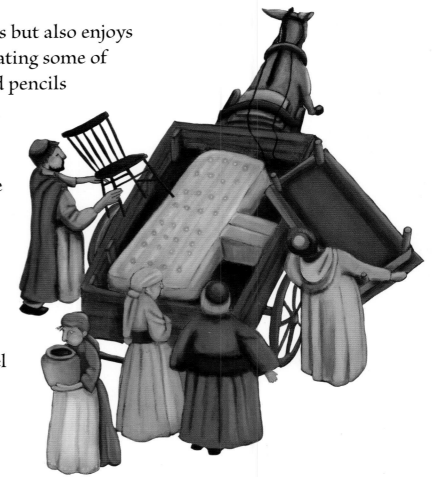